For C.A.
who thought she saw a squirrel on skis.
—J.H.R.

To Manou and Maëlle, my suns.
—P.L.

All rights reserved. Published in the United States by Random House Children's Books,
a division of Random House, Inc., New York.

Beginner Books, Random House, and the Random House colophon are registered trademarks of
Random House, Inc. The Cat in the Hat logo ® and © Dr. Seuss Enterprises, L.P. 1957, renewed
1986. All rights reserved.

Visit us on the Web!
randomhouse.com/kids

Educators and librarians, for a variety of teaching tools, visit us at RHTeachersLibrarians.com

Library of Congress Cataloging-in-Publication Data
Ray, J. Hamilton.
Squirrels on skis / by J. Hamilton Ray ; illustrated by Pascal Lemaitre. — First edition.
  pages cm. — (Beginner books)
Summary: Squirrels on skis take over a town, wreaking havoc among the human residents,
until a girl reporter comes up with a creative solution.
ISBN 978-0-449-81081-1 (trade) — ISBN 978-0-375-97152-5 (lib. bdg.) —
ISBN 978-0-375-98141-8 (ebook)
[1. Stories in rhyme. 2. Squirrels—Fiction. 3. Skis and skiing—Fiction.] I. Lemaitre, Pascal,
illustrator. II. Title.
PZ8.3.R23306Sq 2013 [E]—dc23 2012044919

Printed in the United States of America

10 9 8 7 6 5 4 3

First Edition

Squirrels on Skis

by J. Hamilton Ray
illustrated by Pascal Lemaitre

BEGINNER BOOKS®

A Division of Random House, Inc.

Nobody knew

how the mania grew.

First there was one,

and then there were two.

Three more came gliding
from under the trees.
LOOK! On the hill.
Those are *squirrels on skis!*

Below lay the town,
snow-covered and still.
Not a sound could be heard.
All was silent, until . . .

Swwwishhhh swooped the skiers,
all dressed for play.
Eighty-five squirrels
and more on the way!

And each of them balanced
on two little skis,
wearing muffs on their ears
and pads on their knees.

And all of them holding
two tiny poles,
which they stuck in the snow,
making two tiny holes.

As the townsfolk awoke,
rubbing sleep from their eyes,
they peeked out their windows.
And *what* a surprise!

Wherever they looked
there were squirrels on skis,
skiing in groups
of sixes and threes!

They skied through the green
in the town's center mall.

They skied down the roof
of the great village hall.

They skied by a church
that was filling with people.

One squirrel
climbed up,
and he skied
down the steeple!

They skied through the yards
of the town's well-to-do.
They knocked down a snowman
and garbage can, too.

With a swish and a swoop
and a crackle and crunch,
they had so much fun skiing,
they forgot to eat lunch.

More and more squirrels!
On more and more skis!
Somebody stop them.
Somebody, PLEASE!

So the mayor called a meeting.
But there was no agreeing
on the best way to keep
all those squirrels from skiing.

"Let's ask Stanley Powers,"
said a man dressed in blue.
"He's a pest-control guy.
He'll know what to do."

Mr. Powers stood up
to make his proposal:
"There are *many* good ways
to do squirrel disposal.

"There are poisons and traps . . .
and zappers are nice.
But I'd recommend
my new vacuum device."

"That's cruel!" said a tall man
named Christopher Lunce.
Then *everyone* started
to talk all at once.

The mayor just sighed,
his face full of gloom,
when a voice shouted, "STOP!"
from the back of the room.

It was Sally Sue Breeze.
She could not have been shorter.
But everyone listened,
'cause she's a reporter.

"Haven't you noticed?
These squirrels aren't eating.
They're growing quite thin
from this nonstop competing.

"We have to find out
where they're getting their skis
and stop all this nonsense
before they all freeze."

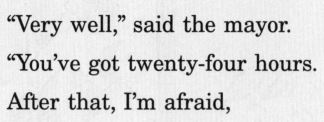

"Very well," said the mayor.
"You've got twenty-four hours.
After that, I'm afraid,
we must call Mr. Powers."

Sally followed the tracks
of the squirrels on skis
back up the hill,
and on through the trees.

And over a bridge
to the edge of the town,
where a very old building
was half falling down.

Above the front door,
against the red bricks,
a faded sign read:
ACME POPSICLE STICKS.

Just at that moment,
a rabbit hopped out.
"SKIS FOR SALE, LADY!"
he said with a shout.

"Ten acorns apiece.

A full pair for twenty.

Step right on up.

As you see, I have plenty."

And there, sure enough,
lay a big pile of sticks.
And right there beside them,
a stack of toothpicks.

"*Toothpicks* for *ski* poles!"
said Sally Sue Breeze.
"And Popsicle sticks
that you've made into skis!"

Then something else caught
little Sally Sue's eye—
a pile of nuts
at least seven feet high.

"So the squirrels have paid you
with nuts, you big cheat!
Now the squirrels have skis,
but they've nothing to eat.

"And they're out of control,"
she said with a frown.
"Those squirrels on skis
are wrecking our town."

"*I* can't be blamed!"
the rabbit protested.
"If you want them to stop,
then have them arrested."

"Ha!" Sally said.
"You know perfectly well
that these toothpicks and sticks
are not yours to sell!

"They were left here last year
when the factory shut down.
Ever since then,
they've belonged to the town."

But an idea was coming
to Sally Sue Breeze—
how to save both the town
and the squirrels on skis.

"I'll forget what you did
if you help make this right.
But we have to work fast,
'cause we haven't much light."

Back in the town,
the poor mayor was pacing.
Around him the squirrels
on skis were still racing.

"Go away, squirrels.
Go away, please!
Mr. Powers is coming!
Go back to your trees!"

Then Powers arrived
with his vacuum device.
He took careful aim.
He was oh so precise.

But before he could start it,
the sky filled with snow.
And off in the distance
there came a warm glow.

The squirrels stopped skiing
to sniff the cold air.
The smell of roast acorns
was now everywhere.

None of them waited
to see what it meant.
They raced out of town
to follow the scent.

They were *so* very hungry
and *so* very cold.
They skied holding hands.
What a sight to behold!

Over one final drift
of the thickening snow,
they skied right on up
to that welcoming glow.

And there stood the rabbit
with sweet Sally Sue,
roasting the nuts
on a big barbecue!

Sally spoke first:
"Come, please take a seat!
Warm your feet by the fire
and have something to eat."

So all of the squirrels
shook off their skis
and sat by the fire
near Sally Sue Breeze.

The white rabbit served them
his favorite treats,
roast acorns and chestnuts
with carrots and beets.

And after a nap,

they wanted to ski.

So Sally Sue told them,
"Please, follow me."

There, 'round the corner,
where the factory once stood,
was a shiny new ski lodge
made of red bricks and wood.

On the front was a sign
painted only that day.
It said:
WELCOME TO BUSHY TAIL
GREAT SKI CHALET.

To the side of the building
were four snowy slopes,
which Sally had marked off
with four colored ropes.

The squirrels jumped up
to put on their skis.
"You must follow the rules!"
called out Sally Sue Breeze.

"Eat three meals a day.
Don't forget to sleep, please.
If you go into town,
you must TAKE OFF YOUR SKIS."

When the mayor heard the plan,
his reaction was swift.
"On behalf of the town,
we shall make this a gift."

So that's how the squirrels
got their own ski chalet.
And they're skiing there still,
to this very day!

As for the rabbit,
you may like to know,
he runs a café,
right there in the snow.

So, if you should be in
this neck of the woods,
be sure to stop by
to sample his goods.

And ask for a seat
by the evergreen trees,
with an excellent view
of those SQUIRRELS ON SKIS!

THE END

J. Hamilton Ray was born in Canada where he learned to ski at the age of two. Since then he has become an accomplished writer and director of children's television, music videos, and documentaries (ABC News). He won two national Emmy Awards for outstanding writing for children. Ray and his wife, the novelist C.A. Belmond, divide their time between Connecticut and France. *Squirrels on Skis* is his first picture book. Visit him at jhamiltonray.com.